The WHO'S WHONicorn of SING-ALONG Unicorns

Kes Gray   Garry Parsons

PUFFIN

Did you know that unicorns **LOVE** to sing?

YAHOOnicorns sing happy songs.

BOOHOOnicorns

sing

sad

songs.

BUCKAROOnicorns sing cowboy songs.

So do **LASSOOnicorns.**

MONSOONicorns like singing in the rain.

SHAMPOOnicorns like singing in the shower.

TUTUnicorns sing . . . AND dance.

GINGGANGGOOLI-GOOLI-GOOLI-GOOnicorns
sing around campfires.

COCKADOODLEDOOnicorns are good at high notes.

MOOnicorns are good at low notes.

PEWnicorns sing hymns and carols.

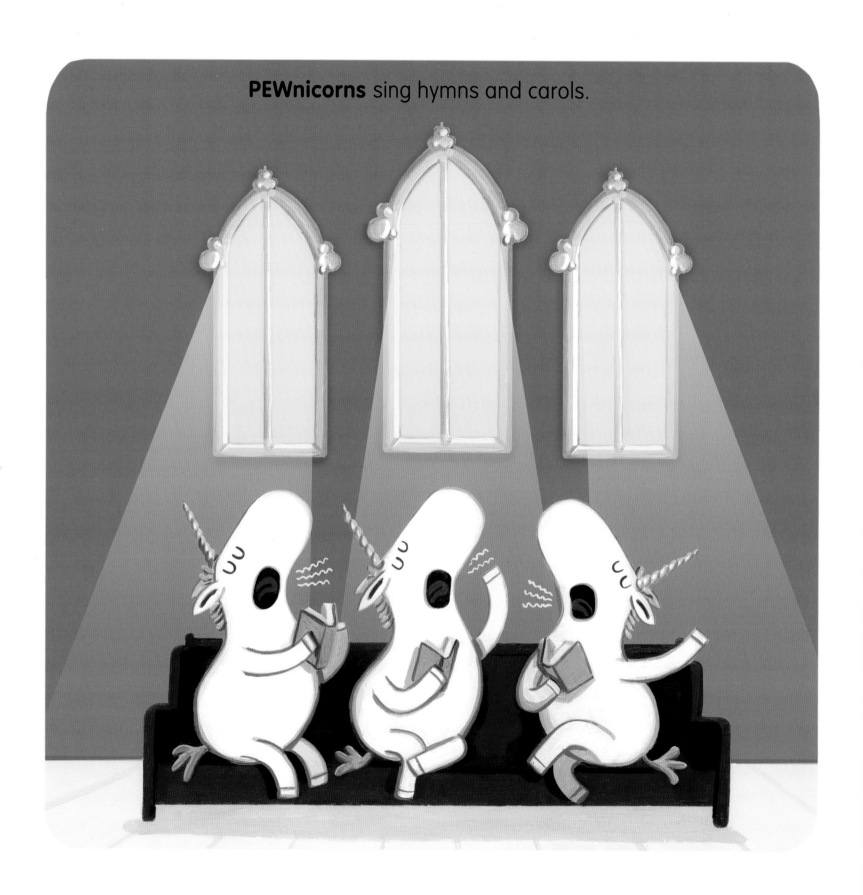

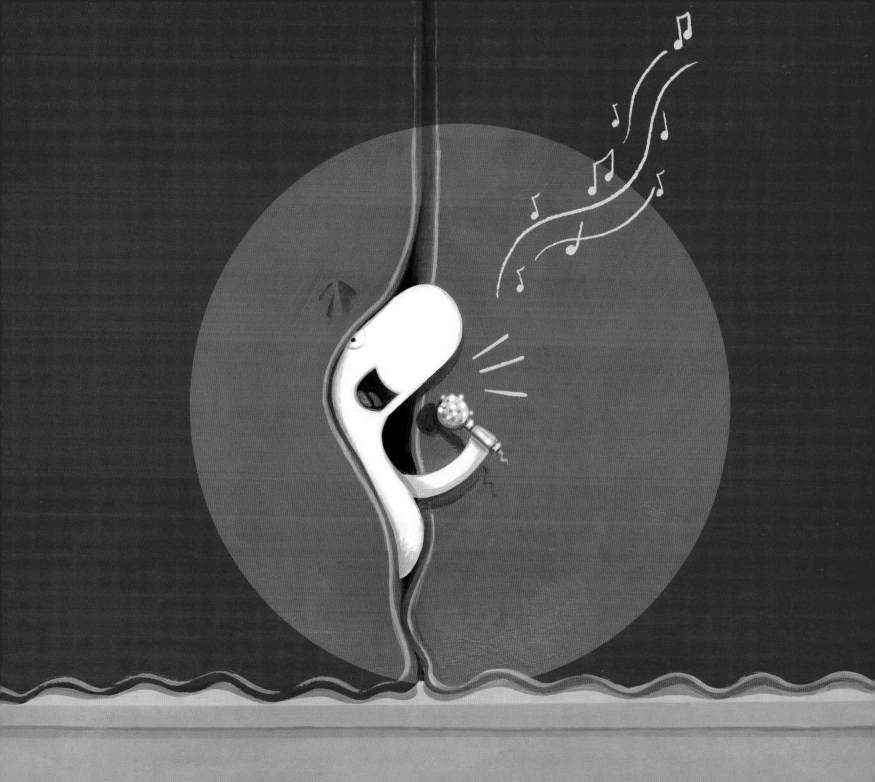

PEEKABOOnicorns sing behind curtains.

IGLOOnicorns sing songs about the North Pole.

DUNEicorns sing songs about deserts.

CROONicorns sing on cruise ships.

WATERLOOnicorns do ABBA tributes.

BLUEnicorns sing the blues.

DOOBYDOOnicorns prefer soul.

BLUESUEDESHOEnicorns sing rock-'n'-roll songs.

AGADOOnicorns sing songs about pushing pineapples from trees.

YODEL-AYE-HEE-HOOnicorns love to yodel.

HAPPYBIRTHDAYTOYOUnicorns only know one song.

BIGMUSICVENUEnicorns attract really large audiences.

THISONEGOESOUTTOYOUnicorns
do requests.

NOCANDOnicorns don't.

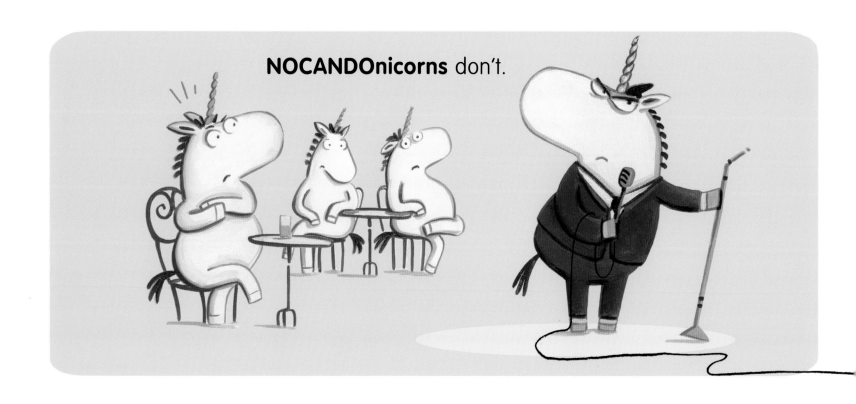

Only one type of unicorn is completely banned from singing.
Can you guess what they are called . . . ?

THE END

(unless you can think of some more!)

For Codunicorn & Kylunicorn – G.P.

Acknowledgements

Lyrics on page 11 adapted from 'I Should Be So Lucky', lyrics by Mike Stock,
Matt Aitken and Pete Waterman, copyright © Mushroom Records Pty. Ltd, 1987

Lyrics on page 11 adapted from 'Moon River', lyrics by Johnny Mercer,
copyright © Famous Music Corporation, 1961 (renewed 1989)

Lyrics on page 14 adapted from 'There's No Business Like Show Business',
lyrics by Irving Berlin, copyright © Irving Berlin Music Company, 1947

Lyrics on page 16 adapted from 'When Will I See You Again',
lyrics by Kenny Gamble and Leon Huff, copyright © CBS, 1973

Lyrics on page 17 adapted from 'Waterloo', lyrics by Benny Andersson,
Björn Ulvaeus and Stig Anderson, copyright © Union Songs AB, 1973

Lyrics on page 20 adapted from 'Blue Suede Shoes', lyrics by Carl Perkins,
copyright © Carl Perkins Music, inc. 1955

Lyrics on page 20 adapted from 'Agadoo', lyrics by Mya Symille, Michael Delancray,
Gilles Péram and Günther Behrle, copyright © Flair Records, 1984.

Every effort has been made to identify and acknowledge copyright holders. The publisher
apologizes for any errors or omissions and if notified of any corrections will make suitable
acknowledgement in future reprints or editions of this book.

Penguin Random House UK

FSC
www.fsc.org
MIX
Paper from
responsible sources
FSC® C018179